T0128755

My Family's Cotillion

My Family's Cotillion

DIETRA REID

MY FAMILY'S COTILLION

iUniverse books may be ordered through booksellers or by contacting:

iUniverse
1663 Liberty Drive
Bloomington, IN 47403
www.iuniverse.com
1-800-Authors (1-800-288-4677)

ISBN: 978-1-4917-7932-3 (sc)
ISBN: 978-1-4917-7933-0 (e)

Print information available on the last page.

iUniverse rev. date: 08/26/2016

1968 Debutantes

THE PRESIDENT'S MESSAGE

MRS. MILEY FRANKLIN
(My mother - Died March 8, 1985)

Tonight we offer our congratulations to you. We wish each of you all the things that make life more abundant. How wonderful it is to share with you and your parents the deep joy of your first achievement in graduating from high school and the making of your debut into society.

Our lives touch you, the young, the beautiful and the hopeful. You brought something into our lives by sharing your dreams with us. You gave us new hope. The future of the world lies in the hands of the young, for you are the leaders of tomorrow.

I implore you to prepare yourselves and find a place and serve humanity in the best way possible. Do not underestimate any position because anything that is worth doing at all is worth doing well. Give all that you are capable of giving. Go as far as you can and when you get there, I promise you that you will see further. The rainbow is just beyond the clouds. Watch for the silver lining.

The hour of decision is at hand. The world awaits you and we need your constructive ideas to help us to make this world a better place.

MY FAMILY'S COTILLION

A screenplay by Ms. Dietra Reid based on the real
cotillions by The Arista Society of Queens.

Interior of NYC Office Building/Plush office/
Present day-Man Holding Picture-
He stands near his desk. He wipes
his eyes as the phone rings.

MILES KENNEDY(mid 40's, news journalist)

Hello, yes I am working on a story for next week.

He sits down. The light is close up on the
black and white picture he his holding.
He closes his eyes as he remembers,

The next day. The exterior of a hospital.
People going in and out of it.

Miles Kennedy entering the room of a patient,

MILES leans closer to his mother.

MILES

What?

SUSAN KENNEDY(mid 60's. dying of cancer)

Miles, your father is black. We met at C University in New York as students there. We dated And eventually married. (SUSAN paused for a moment looking out the window)

I could not handle the problems of being an interracial couple. Strangers said such ugly things to us. I loved him very much.

MILES

What?

SUSAN

I asked for a divorce after leaving him because of that. I didn't find out I was pregnant with you until after I left. When I went back home my father was sick and then he died soon. My mother was diagnosed soon after with Cancer and died too. Son, I'm so sorry to tell you this now. Please forgive me. (she burst into tears)

MILES (there was an intense shock
on his face, quiet for a minute)

Mom, you are telling me now that I'm black?

SUSAN

I'm telling you that you are half black. But no one has to
know. You've been passing for all white your whole life.
I'm sorry I didn't tell you sooner. Please don't be mad at
me. Your father doesn't know anything about you. He
doesn't know you exist. I heard he made it as a journalist
somewhere in NY just like you. Or the other way around.

MILES

What happened to him?

SUSAN

Your father remarried a year after our divorce. Son, please
don't hate me. I made a terrible mistake out of fear of
others. Fear of how my parents would react. Fear of how
society would treat you. I was a coward. Don't hate me.

MILES (put his head down, took a deep breath)

Mom, I don't hate you. I just don't understand how you
could have not told me before.

SUSAN

I regretted that. I went back twice to tell your father but didn't. The second time I saw his new wife was pregnant.

MILES

But mom, he still could have been my father.

SUSAN

I know that now son. I realize how selfish that was. When you see him it will be your decision whether to tell him about you or not.

MILES

What a horrible decision to have to make?

SUSAN (putting her face in her hands)

I know son and I am sorry. I just wanted you to know you had a good man as a father. He would be so proud of you now, just as I am. I tried to make it up to you by working hard to give you the best. Son, I was scarred, young and stupid. After, when you think of me don't judge me to harshly. Do you hate me now?

MILES

No mom, I don't hate you. You did give me the best.

SUSAN

Thank you for that son. There is a picture in the back of my closet of your father. It was one of him being in a cotillion his senior year of high school with the Arista Society of Queens before I met. I'm so tired son.

PRESENT TIME AGAIN-Back at MILES office in NY-Miles looking at the picture again. He picks up his phone.

MILES (makes an in-house call)

KENNY JOHNSON (you hear him but don't see him)

Mr. Kennedy can I help you with something?

MILES

Yes, I need everything on the "Arista Society of Queens". It was a black cotillion organization that had one of its cotillions at the Hotel back in around 1968.

KENNY

Okay I will get right on it.

MILES

Thanks

MILES

How long do you think it will take?

KENNY

Do you know if any of the organizers are still alive?

MILES

No, I don't

When do you need it?

MILES

Tomorrow morning.

KENNY

You will have it.

MILES

Thanks again Kenny

KENNY

You okay Mr. Kennedy

MILES

Yes, why?

KENNY

Because I never remember you ever thanking me before for getting you research or for anything.

MILES

Oh, well I have to go.

Miles straightened up his office to leave for the night. He looked at the picture of his father one more time. He left the building. He got into his car in the parking garage. Then he pulled off.

Miles House-Exterior-Nighttime-He walks to his front door and goes in.

Next day-Exterior Miles Office-Morning. Miles walks over to his desk. He sits in his chair. The Secretary walks in thru the open door of his office.

SECRETARY

Are you all right Mr. Kennedy?

MILES

Yes, I didn't see you come in.

Secretary

If you need a listening ear, I'm here. You sure let me vent about my kids to you. You probably won't want to have any now. (She laughs).

MILES

They're not that bad. I just don't have a definite story yet for the February issue.

SECRETARY

Don't worry you will. See you later. (She leaves the office)

Silence for a few minutes. Miles looks thru past writing notes. Then the interoffice buzzer rings.

KENNY

I have the information you wanted, Mr. Kennedy.

MILES

Right on time.

KENNY

Yeah, I could use those words for my next review. I'm trying to get the full time position as research assistant instead of full time mail boy and part time research boy.

MILES

You got it. I will put it in writing for your boss.

KENNY

I was just kidding Mr. Kennedy.

MILES

Yeah, a little maybe. But not about the job.

KENNY

Now, I have to go because something is...wrong.

MILES typed up a recommendation letter for KENNY himself on his computer. MILES buzzed the SECRETARY.

MILES

Hello, when you get a chance can you retype a recommendation letter I did for KENNY? His review I think is coming up soon. I just emailed it to you.

SECRETARY

Sure, but are you okay?

MILES

Why, KENNY asked me the same thing. Did I ever
mistreat him or something? Did I act prejudice or
something?

SECRETARY

No MILES, nothing like that. You are one of the most
unprejudiced white man I know. It's just that since your
mother died you've seem to take a personal interest in
the African-American employees here. Before you were
always polite and spoke but I guess you felt you had
nothing in common for the conversation to go any
further. Maybe your mother's passing has made you a
more reaching out human being?

MILES

Maybe but if I don't get a idea for the two-thirty meeting
I don't know how anything Mr. Kyler will be?

SECRETARY

Yeah, that's a fact. Talk to you later. (Interoffice phone
off.)

MILES looks down at the fax information KENNY just
faxed him for a minute. MILES picks up his phone.

MILES

Hello, can I speak to Mr. Giles please?

Ms. GILES's GRANDSON

Yes, can I help you?

Hello, my name is Mr. MILES KENNEDY. I'm a journalist with the NEW MAGAZINE. I would like to do a story on "THE ARISTA SOCIETY OF QUEENS. I understand you were their photographer for the 1968 cotillion held at the B HOTEL?

GRANDSON

How do I know you are legit? There is a lot of fraud going on?

MILES

Okay, I'll have my information sent to you on our official raised letterhead delivered to you first class. You can call me back after you receive it.

GRANDSON

You sound legit. Hold on. I will get my grandfather.

Mr. GILES (hear him but not see him)

Hello, my grandson said you're from the NEW Magazine and want to do a story on "The Arista Society of Queens?"

MILES

Yes, that's correct. How are you Mr. Giles?

Mr. Giles

I am enjoying my retirement.

MILES

That's good. I'm trying to get in contact with the cotillion's president or some of it's other officers.

Mr. Giles

Sorry to say all of them have passed away. But Ms. Castle, the president's daughter is still alive. I took the pictures for her daughter's middle school graduation.

MILES

Is it possible for you to give me her number?

Mr. Giles

Sure can. Her first name is Deanna. Her number is 914-636-6622.

MILES

Thank you very much. Could I interview you about the Cotillion?

Mr. GILES

Talk to Deanna first. If she say's yes to the story then you sure can.

MILES hangs up the phone. He looks at his watch. He walks to his boss's office. MILES's boss's door is open. He knocks.

Mr. KYLER (MILES's BOSS)

MILES come on in.

MILES sits on the coach. He takes a deep breath.

Mr. KYLER

MILES you're right on time.

MILES

Yeah, I try to be.

Mr. KYLER

Come on, why so formal. You look better than yesterday. I know it's been hard on you losing your mother and work deadlines over the last few months. But as you know the magazine waits for no one to heal. Do you have an idea for your February cover story?

MILES

Yes, I just came up with it this morning. It's the story of a regular, hardworking, African-American family from the south who "made it" successfully in the north wanting to give back. They're not rich though. They live from paycheck to paycheck like everybody else. The start the

Arista Society of Queens that host scholarship cotillions for black students in the Bronx, Queens, and Manhattan. Their cotillions are at hotels like the B Hotel and the W Astoria in downtown Manhattan. Black owned businesses and unions were the kids are from help out by buying advertisement space in their journal and buying tickets. The King and Queen of the cotillion receive college scholarships.–1968

Mr. KYLER

How's that a story? They were a lot of cotillions back then both white and black?

MILES

But this family wanted the students to feel they mattered and were valuable. They wanted to dignify these kids and in the process their community to in celebration.

Mr. KYLER

Where did you get all that from?

MILES (laughs and tries to compose himself)

Well, I talked to the photographer of the cotillion back then. I heard it in his voice.

Mr. KYLER

Well, do some light research on it. Since it will be black history month. Maybe we can do it if we do not have any other story.

MILES (he got up and started walking out.)

Okay

MILES walked back to his office. He looked out the window and took a deep breath before picking up his phone.

MILES

Hello, my name is MILES KENNEDY. I am a writer for The New Magazine. I would like to do a story on your family's cotillion sponsored by your "The Arista Society of Queens back in the late 1960's that gave college scholarships to high school seniors.

DEANNA CASTLE(on phone not see her, mid 50's.)

Who are you again and what do you want?

MILES

I'm MILES KENNEDY and I'm a writer from the New Magazine I would like to do a story about your family's cotillion.

DEANNA

And how did you get my name and number?

MILES

From Mr. GILES, the cotillion's photographer.

DEANNA

How do I know you are legit?

MILES

You could call information to get the phone number for the New MAGAZINE.

Then you could call the office and ask to speak to my boss. Then ask for verification be sent to you about me on our raised letterhead company paper.

DEANNA

Okay, I might do that.

MILES

Thank You Ms. Castle

INT-DEANNA CASTLE's HOUSE- She has an old three bedroom, ranch house in White Plains, NY DEANNA answered MILES call while she was in her bedroom. She walks to the kitchen to make Breakfast. DEANNA's house phone rings. DEANNA answers it.

DEANNA

Hello

HESSA (DEANNA's thirteen year
old daughter-hear her only)

Mom, the bus is late. I'm hungry.

DEANNA

Hey, a writer from NY wants to do an article on your grandmother's cotillion.

HESSA

Not being mean Mom, but why that's was so long ago.

DEANNA

Because it was an accomplishment. It was to teach the kids, minority kids in some poor neighborhoods and some not that they were somebody too.

HESSA

Okay Mom, here comes my bus. Bye

DEANNA turned the coffee pot off. She went upstairs to take shower and get dressed. After she finished the phone rang. She answered it in her bedroom on 2nd floor.

DEANNA

Hello

OLIVIA Johnson (hear her but not see her)

Hello, how are you? I'm surprised to catch you home this morning.

DEANNA

Yeah, me too. My heart was fluttering this morning. So I didn't call in to get a substitute assignment today.

OLIVIA

Did you take your medicine? How's Hessa?

DEANNA

Yes, I took it before breakfast. HESSA said she wasn't hungry this morning. I tried to get her to eat, no success. Do you know she called back while waiting at the bus stop complaining because she was hungry?

OLIVIA

Teenagers. But you know you have a good kid though.

DEANNA

Yeah, she is. Aunt Olivia, a man saying he was from the New Magazine called. He wants to do a story about our family cotillion

OLIVIA

Check him out first.

DEANNA

I will.

OLIVIA

Are you going to let him do the story if he's legit?

DEANNA

I haven't decided yet. First I have to have his story verified.

OLIVIA

Let me know what you decide; How does HESSA feel about it?

DEANNA

As usual she doesn't understand why anyone would be interested in events that old.

OLIVIA

That's a modern day teenager for you. Talk to you.

DEANNA (laughing)

Talk to you again soon Aunt Olivia.

DEANNA hung up the phone. It rang within the minute.

DEANNA

Hello

HESSA

How's your vacation day going, mom? Can we have Chinese for diner?

DEANNA

What vacation day? I have laundry to catch up on. We are having pork chops, rice and string beans for diner HESSA.

HESSA

Okay Mom

DEANNA walked to the basement to do laundry. She cleaned the house up to the time HESSA came home from school.

HESSA (walked in the front door)

Hi Mom

DEANNA (walked out of the living room into Kitchen)

Hi honey. How was school?

HESSA

Same O, Same O. There's a trip to France this spring.

DEANNA

That's great. Which class?

HESSA (agitated voice)

French class, Mom

DEANNA

It could have been in another class. Aren't you glad you stuck with it?

HESSA (laughing)

No

DEANNA (gives HESSA a hug)

Diner will be ready in about a hour.

HESSA (walking upstairs)

Okay. I'll be upstairs in my room.

HESSA goes into her room and turns her computer on. She works on her homework. DEANNA goes back into the kitchen to finish the diner. In about an hour she calls HESSA for diner.

HESSA (yells)

HESSA, diner is ready.

DEANNA

Okay Mom, I'll be right down.

They eat diner talking about their day. Then they watch TV for a while.

DEANNA (gives her a hug)

Goodnight HESSA, I'm going to bed a little earlier tonight. See you in the morning.

HESSA

Goodnight Mom

INT-CASTLE'S KITCHEN. NEXT MORNING-HESSA is making herself a bowl of cereal. She looks at the kitchen clock on the counter. It reads 7:30a.m. She walks upstairs to her mother's bedroom. She knocks on the door.

HESSA (knocking on the door)

Mom, are you all right?

DEANNA (In her bed)

Yes, come in. What time is it?

HESSA

7:30 mom. Are you all right? I'm getting ready to leave for school. You usually always beat me to the kitchen in the mornings.

DEANNA

I know, just tired today baby. My heart worked a little to hard yesterday. Have a good day at school.

HESSA

Yeah, get some rest mom.

DEANNA got out of the bed very slowly. She went into to bathroom. She took a shower. She got dressed. She walked downstairs and put the coffee pot on. She picked up the phone.

DEANNA (sounding sleepy)

Hello information. Can I have the number for The New Magazine in Manhattan, New York please?

Operator

212-555-1212

DEANNA pulled out her family album in her bedroom. She looked at the wedding picture of her grandparents. She thought of when they got married back in 1928 in Mobile, Alabama.

Outside-Small country house in rural Mobile, Alabama-1928-Family seeing newlywed off on their honeymoon.

1st Friend (woman)

Congratulations, come back safe from your honeymoon.

2nd Friend

Don't eat too much in Louisiana now.

Interior-1929-Young couple's house. Wife holding a baby. Pregnant with another.

DEANNA's GRANDFATHER

There's no work here except at the docks. I don't know how to do that work. I'm a ball player. I'm looking but can't find no other work around here except that.

DEANNA's GRANDMOTHER

I could take in a little wash to help us along. That wouldn't be to much.

DEANNA'S GRANDFATHER

No wife of mine gonna do no white woman's wash.

1930- Downtown colonial house, Mobile, Alabama-DEANNA's GRANDMOTHER carrying a baby knocking on the door.

DEANNA's GRANDMOTHER

Hello, Mrs. Smith. I'm here to see about the maid job

Mrs. SMITH

Oh yes. Come in. Cute baby (she opens the front door for her)

DEANNA's GRANDMOTHER

I worked for the Browns on Dolphin Island right out of high school. And here is there number.

Mrs. SMITH

Well, I'm willing to give anyone a chance. When can you start?

DEANNA's GRANDMOTHER

I can start tomorrow. Will I have room and board here Mrs.?

Mrs. SMITH

Yes you will plus a small cash pay. You will also have to take care of our daughter. She is 18 months. Do you have someone good to raise your daughter? Where's her father?

DEANNA's GRANDMOTHER

He went back to playing for the black baseball league. We're divorced. I could find someone to look after her but I kind of want to keep her close. Can I raise her here too? You can take away the cash pay.

Mrs. SMITH

Well, that will be more work for you, two children. And me and my husband might have more. You would have to do all the cooking, washing and cleaning too.

DEANNA's GRANDMOTHER

I can do it Mamm. With my daughter here I'll do a good job.

Mrs. SMITH

Okay, I'll give anyone a chance.

A year later-Kitchen of Mrs. SMITH's kitchen. Mrs. SMITH's daughter playing on the floor with the pots and pans with DEANNA'S Grandmother's daughter (her mother)

Mrs. Smith walked into the kitchen. She looked at the toddlers playing on the floor together and got angry.

Mrs. SMITH

HENRIETTA (DEANNA's GRANDMOTHER's name) you have to make sure they know what it means to be colored in this country and what it means not to be. They are not equal you know. You know I've been more than fair with you. But no since setting your own child up for heartbreak thinking that she is equal to my Mary. You are a good worker and a good woman. Your daughter will probably be just like you. Maybe your girl can be the worker in my daughter's house when they grow up. It was all right for them to play together when they were little babies but it's time to separate them now. You understand? It's just the way it is.

HENRIETTA (holding her breath)

Yes Mame

I know you would. I knew you wouldn't be like those trouble makers from the north coming down here trying to change things. It's how it's always been that's all. When you needed somewhere to work, live at and raise your baby, I let you do it here.

HENRIETTA

You did Mamae

Mrs. SMITH

When you needed a half day off to go to your cousin's funeral I gave it to you and let you cook diner a few minutes late.

HENRIETTA

Yes, thank you for that Mame.

Mrs. SMITH

See we understand each other. (she walked out the kitchen)

HENRIETTA turned away from the toddlers on the floor. She put a dishcloth in her mouth to drown out her screams as tears rolled softly down her face.

A year later-HENRIETTA's daughter was now 4 years old. -KITCHEN of the Mrs. SMITH

MILEY (HENRIETTA's daughter)

Mama, what's wrong?

HENRIETTA

Remember to not look white people in the eye. To say yes madam to the woman and yes sir to the men.

Back to present day-DEANNA House

DEANNA went into the kitchen to make some breakfast. The phone rang.

OLIVIA

Hi, how are you?

DEANNA

I'm okay, Aunt Olivia.

OLIVIA

You sound distracted, is everything all right?

DEANNA

Yes. I was looking at Grandma and Grandpa's wedding picture. Wasn't something how it ended up?

OLIVIA

Yeah, you're grandmother wouldn't let us raise your mother while she worked in that house. But my brother should have stayed and found some other kind of work. But in the end it all worked out. Look how your grandmother was able to raise your mother and see her thru high school working days at a white woman's house having her own house eventually. Then your mother married your father and they moved to NY while he was in his third year of college. She going to college too. No telling what hard work and determination can do.

DEANNA

Yeah. And then my mother going to get grandfather when he was sick and taking care of him until he died.

OLIVIA

Didn't he ask your forgiveness before he died or your mother's making Peace?

DEANNA

Yes.

OLIVIA

Did you decide to do the article about the cotillion?

DEANNA

I didn't get the confirmation yet.

OLIVIA

Let me know when you get it. I have to go. Bye

DEANNA

Bye

The phone rings again. DEANNA answers it in the living room sitting down.

DEANNA

Hello

HESSA

Hi mom, I'm staying after school for coach class. Can you pick me up at four?

DEANNA

Okay, what entrance will you be at?

HESSA

I'll be at the main entrance. Thanks Mom. Bye

DEANNA

Bye

DEANNA put the phone down. She ate her breakfast. She went to check the mail box. It had a letter from the New Magazine She opened the letter. She made diner and did a load of laundry. At 3:30p.m. she got into her car and drove to HESSA's School. She parked in front.

HESSA (jumping into the car)

Hi Mom thanks.

DEANNA

Hi you're welcome. How was school?

HESSA

It was okay. Same o, same o.

DEANNA

Did coach class help?

HESSA

Yeah a little. Can I put the music on?

DEANNA

Yeah, as long as you don't blast it.

HESSA

DEANNA drive to the house. HESSA went to her room to start on her homework. DEANNA went to the kitchen to finish making diner. Two hours late DEANNA and HESSA sat down for diner.

HESSA

Mom, the pork chops aren't bad.

DEANNA

Thanks for the around the way compliment I think. (Laughing)

HESSA (laughing)

Yeah

DEANNA

How would you feel if I agreed to let the New Magazine do an article on the family cotillion?

HESSA

Mom. Nothing personal against you but that's old history.
Mom if it makes you happy, go for it.

DEANNA

Oh HESSA, I can't get thru to you about how special that
was considering the year

It was in.

HESSA

Sorry Mom, I don't see how it's important now.

DEANNA

Maybe one day you will.

HESSA

Mom, I love you though.

DEANNA

I love you too.

They finish eating diner. They wash the dishes together.
HESSA starts to walk upstairs but looks back.

HESSA

Mom, I'm going to call Mary to see if she can help me with some of my homework.

DEANNA

Okay, tell her I said hello. I'm going to do some work on the computer.

DEANNA went into their spare bedroom. She got on the computer in there. Then she picked up a family album in there. DEANNA smiled at some of the pictures. HESSA walked in.

DEANNA

Your grandfather met your grandmother at the ice cream store she worked in. She worked there after school in high school her third year. He was in his last year of high school on his way to college. They started dating. They got married as soon as your mother finished high school. They lived with his aunt in NY while he went finished up college.

DEANNA

HESSA

I know Mom

DEANNA

Did I tell you how hard they worked to go to school work and save up for their own apartment at first. Then houses late on?

HESSA

Yes

DEANNA

Did I tell you how much they loved living in the "Sugar Hill" section of Harlem back in their day, 1950's?

HESSA

Yes Mom, you told me that too. How they loved going to the A on amateur night. How on Sunday's some avenue, I think Seventh Avenue was a walking fashion show.

DEANNA

I'm going to faint, you do listen.

HESSA

When I went to central park last year with my friends it wasn't exactly the way grandma described it though.

DEANNA

Yeah, I thought the same way when I went long ago to with my friends. It was nice but I couldn't see staying there until midnight listening to people play live Spanish music and feeling safe today.

HESSA

Did you see my favorite jeans?

DEANNA

Did you look in the laundry bin in the basement?

HESSA (leaving the room)

No

DEANNA (yelling)

Did you find it?

HESSA (yelling back)

Yes

DEANNA took out the suitcase of cotillion things. She smiled to herself. She put them on the chair. HESSA walked into the room.

HESSA

So Mom, are you going to do the interview?

DEANNA

I haven't decided yet. If I say yes I want to make sure it's done in a respectful and dignified way.

HESSA

Don't you get to preview it first?

DEANNA

Maybe

HESSA (leaving the room)

Okay, Mom

DEANNA put all the cotillion material back in the suitcase. She put the suitcase back in the closet. She walked downstairs to the kitchen. She picked up the phone.

DEANNA (on the phone)

Hello, this is Ms. Castle. Can I speak to Mr. Miles Kennedy please?

MILES KENNEDY (in his office)

Hello, this is MILES KENNEDY. How are you?

DEANNA

I'm good thank you. I have decided to let your magazine do our family cotillion story.

MILES

Great, what's your work schedule like for the rest of the week?

DEANNA

I have a work assignment for tomorrow but I'm free on Thursday.

MILES

Good, I'll have a company sedan pick you up at 9:00a.m. We can go over the details here at the office. Then we can celebrate at your favorite restaurant here in Manhattan. Sound good?

DEANNA

My lawyer said just to fax over the final contract to him for review before I sign it. Is that okay?

MILES

Yes. That won't be a problem. See you on Wednesday. Bye.

DEANNA

Bye

The next day. Exterior of DEANNA's house. Early morning sunrise. DEANNA walks into her kitchen. Buzz the phone rings.

DEANNA

Hello

OLIVIA (hear her but not see her)

Hi, are you feeling better?

DEANNA

Hi, yes I am Aunt Olivia. I'm going to work today.

OLIVIA

That's good. Did you decide on the cotillion story yet?

DEANNA

Yes, I'm going to do it. And the interesting thing is HESSA helped me to decide.

OLIVIA

Kids sure do surprise you, huh?

DEANNA

Yeah, they sure do.

OLIVIA

I'm going to talk to you later. Take it slow until you feel all the way better. Bye

DEANNA

Bye

DEANNA hangs up the phone. DEANNA starts making breakfast

HESSA walks into the kitchen.

HESSA

Mom, I have to do a oral report on a historical event for black history month in February. Was there any famous African-Americans in the cotillion?

DEANNA

Yes there was. The mistress of ceremonies for the cotillion one year ended up becoming the first black woman ambassador the state of NY. Really, for any state.

HESSA

What do you mean, state ambassador?

DEANNA

It was a position started after the Civil War and phased out after the Vietnam War. It was a volunteer position appointed by the governor of each state. It was used to try to pull the states together in a nonparty, nonpolitical way after the gulf of ending slavery.

HESSA

What was her name?

DEANNA

Mrs. Carlene Chism

HESSA

What a name. How long after the cotillion was she elected?

DEANNA

She was appointed about three months after the cotillion in September, 1968.

HESSA

What was she like?

DEANNA

She was beautiful, and dedicated to helping people better their lives. She especially tried to help woman and children who were poor.

HESSA

Do you have any pictures of her?

DEANNA

Yes, lots of them.

HESSA

Is she still alive?

DEANNA

Yes

HESSA

How did she help people?

DEANNA

She helped start the pre wic and head start program in poor neighborhoods thru out NYC by working with local mom and pop supermarkets. Also, she got local doctors to volunteer at newly formed free clinics in the area.

HESSA

Why isn't any of this in the history books at school?

DEANNA

That's a good question. But I don't have the answer.

HESSA

I'm going to ask my teacher if I can do the cotillion for my oral report.

DEANNA

Are you now interested in the cotillion?

HESSA

Maybe

They finished eating breakfast. DEANNA went to the spare bedroom. She got out the the suitcase of cotillion things. She brought it down to the kitchen. She gave the souvenir journal to HESSA.

HESSA (looking thru the journal at the table)

What is a lady in waiting?

DEANNA

I believe they were the older ladies in King Arthur's court who looked after the princesses and maybe the Queen.

HESSA

Is that a lady in waiting whose putting the crown on the Queen in this picture?

DEANNA

Yes it is. She is also your cousin. Aunt Coretta Jones. She was my father's first cousin. She was one of my favorite relatives growing up. She used strong words but had a heart of gold. It was a contradiction.

HESSA

Why do you say that she had a heart of gold?

DEANNA

Because in her housing project in lower Manhattan near Houston street, next to China Town she helped immigrant woman get food and milk for their children. She couldn't stand to see people be without basic things. She became ill later in her life but kept her joy, sense of humor and strength.

HESSA

What do you mean?

DEANNA

In my teens I went to see her in the intensive care after one of her surgeries. She was asleep. She had so many wires and tubes coming from into and out of her body I almost fainted on seeing her. She woke up and saw my face. She calmly told me that I had to be strong. That if I ever woke up in a situation like hers, that I had to stay calm. She made me feel better.

HESSA

She said that hooked up to all those wires in the intensive care?

DEANNA

Yeah, she was fighting for her life and she showed me such love.

HESSA

That was something.

DEANNA

Yeah

HESSA

Any more relatives in the cotillion?

DEANNA

I told you this before it was your cousin Carol Dianne, your cousin Emanuel, your Aunt Olivia, Your Aunt Hatie, Your uncle Terrance, your uncle Lee, Your cousin Eugenia too.

HESSA (she puts on her backpack)

To many relatives, I'm going to be late for school. Bye.

DEANNA (laughing)

Yeah, we do have a lot of relatives. Bye have a good day at school.

HESSA (leaving out the door)

Yeah, I'll try.

The phone rings. DEANNA answers it.

AUNT OLIVIA (hear her but don't see her)

Hello

DEANNA

Hello, Aunt Olivia how are you?

AUNT OLIVIA

Good is everything all right with you?

DEANNA

Yes, guess whose interested in the cotillion now?

AUNT OLIVIA

Why your daughter of course.

DEANNA

How did you know?

AUNT OLIVIA

Because children never cease to surprise you. Just when you think about counting them out on something they come thru.

DEANNA

She's going to ask her teacher can she do her oral report for black history month of the cotillion.

AUNT OLIVIA

She has all the information right there.

DEANNA

And she can go with the editor and I to interview people involved in the cotillion.

AUNT OLIVIA

Maybe she will see what your mother and others tried to do for the young people of their generation.

DEANNA

That would be something.

AUNT OLIVIA

Yeah, after all the years you tried to get her interested in it. DEANNA I have to go. I'll talk to you soon. Bye

DEANNA

Okay, AUNT OLIVIA, Bye.

DEANNA leaves the house for work. She gets into her car. The scene ends.

The sun is setting. DEANNA pulls into her driveway. She goes into her house. She goes into the kitchen. A few minutes later HESSA walks into the house.

HESSA

Hi mom, my teacher said I can do the report on the cotillion. Can I look thru the book again?

DEANNA (picks up the book from the table)

Sure here. I was looking thru it myself after I got home from work.

HESSA

Mom, why did grandma and the other relatives do the cotillion?

DEANNA

That's a long story. But I guess basically they never forgot how hard it was for them growing up. They wanted to give back. This house we're living in now after my divorce from your father they bought after years of hard work and saving.

HESSA

I know you told me.

DEANNA

I remember as a young child going with my mom to run down tenement buildings in the city to talk to high school seniors and their parents about being in the cotillion.

Some single mothers were reluctant I realized much later to let their daughters or sons be in it. It was as if they thought they wouldn't be treated well.

DEANNA

Some girls didn't want to wear a dress.

HESSA

What did grandma do?

DEANNA

Well, on one occasion before grandma could do anything
I told the girl she had to be in the cotillion. I told her she
would look so pretty in it.

HESSA

How old were you?

DEANNA

About six

HESSA

Did you get into trouble?

DEANNA

Well, your grandmother gave me one of her famous looks.

HESSA

Did the girl end up being in the cotillion?

DEANNA

HESSA, I don't even know.

HESSA

Oh mom. A lot of debutants have only their mother's listed under their name.

DEANNA

Yeah, I noticed that after my own separation.

HESSA

Why

DEANNA

I don't know maybe grandma especially reached out to single parent families like how she was raised and ones having a hard time. Grandma didn't have it easy growing up.

HESSA

I know mom, you told me.

DEANNA

Just wanted you to know hard work does pay off. I'm going to be bed early. I'm kind of tired tonight. Diner is on top of the stove. (leaves the room)

HESSA

Goodnight mom.

INT-MILES KENNEDY's apartment. MILES is sitting down at his dining room table. He is looking down at the picture of his father in a tuxedo with cumber band in front of the W Astoria Hotel. He thinks back to what his mother tells him before she dies.

Int-Hospital patient room. MILES's mother SUSAN is hooked up to heart monitor.

SUSAN (raspy voice)

Son, your father and I met in college. We were in the same journalism class at C??? University in New York City. We became good friends at first. Then we started dating.

MILES

Was it a mixed racial group?

SUSAN

No, the small city I grew up here in Iowa had no blacks living anywhere near it. It would have been worse than in NY.

MILES

How did both of your parents feel about you dating?

SUSAN

Your father's parents were very supportive but concerned. I didn't tell my parents.

MILES

Where did you go on your first date?

SUSAN

We went to hear a guest speaker at our journalism club?

MILES

How did my father ask you out?

SUSAN

He was shy at first. He came up to me one day before the club meeting. He said "Susan, are you going to the hear the guest speaker tomorrow night?" When I told him yes he relaxed. Then he said "Would you like to go with me?"

MILES

Did you say yes right away?

SUSAN

Yes, I sure did. Your father was not only handsome, smart but a nice guy.

MILES

Did you go anywhere else on that first date besides the club meeting?

SUSAN

Yes, we did. He asked me was I hungry? When I said yes we took the subway to Harlem.

MILES

Wasn't that dangerous for a biracial couple back then?

SUSAN

I don't know anybody that night seemed to take any notice. We went to a soul food place on 125th street near Lennox Ave. We got a few surprised looks or turned heads but that's all. That was the first time I tasted corn bread and greens.

MILES

Is that when you met my father's family?

SUSAN

No, it was a few months later. His aunt was having a Sunday Family Diner. She asked him to bring his girlfriend. Your father's mother had been asking to meet me.

MILES

How did that go?

SUSAN

I was nervous at first about meeting them from the moment I woke up that Sunday morning. But his family was nice and very sophisticated about racial issues.

MILES

Did they change when you two got serious?

SUSAN

No, but they were very worried for us about other people's reactions.

MILES

Why?

SUSAN

It was early 1970's. All the public schools in the south weren't even all segregated yet. In some parts of the south Jim Crow laws were still enforced. Sometimes men were still being found hung in a tree in the deep, Deep South.

MILES

I didn't realize that all of that was still going on then.

SUSAN

The northern states were safer for black people but
there still was some prejudice there too. It was just more
invisible.

MILES

Like how?

SUSAN

Your father told me like not getting the job you were
qualified to get but it went to a white person less qualified.

MILES

How else?

SUSAN

Like not being rented an apartment or being allowed to
buy a certain house in certain neighborhood.

MILES

So, the discrimination in the northern states was more
financial?

SUSAN

Son, your father's family said it made it harder for blacks
to get basic needs met.

MILES

How?

SUSAN

In certain parts of New York City back then the rent was double if you were black.

MILES

What?

SUSAN

If you were black and qualified to buy a house the down payment was doubled the amount of a white person.

MILES

And how about the mortgage?

SUSAN

The same

MILES

Mom, wasn't that against the constitution and bill of rights. Was this against blacks only?

SUSAN

No, your father's mother told me her mother said there use to be signs up "No dogs and no Jews". And it was said that some other immigrants had it hard to due to prejudice

MILES

That's horrible.

SUSAN

In school I met kids of parents who lived thru the holocaust. They came to the US for a new start. But some were spit on.

MILES

So this is what my father's family was worried about for you?

SUSAN

Your father's mother was worried about us being able to rent an apartment. She wondered how our marriage would affects our jobs or careers later.

MILES

Why?

SUSAN

Even some very liberal people thought biracial dating was fine. But biracial marriage was a totally different thing. If your boss or the owner of the company hated biracial marriages then you could lose your job.

MILES

Just like that?

SUSAN

Just like that. So when you're father told his parents he wanted to marry me, they were concerned.

MILES

How did your parents take it when you told them?

SUSAN

I never told them.

MILES

Why?

SUSAN

Because of what my mother had told me before I met your father. She said "I heard young people in the north are dating black people. Maybe they are experimenting. But I believe it is wrong to marry someone from another race."

MILES

How did your father feel?

SUSAN

He told me that parents should disown any child who married outside of his race.

MILES

When did he say that?

SUSAN

Right after your father and I started dating.

MILES

How did you feel?

SUSAN

I was devastated. I tried to call back to talk to them about your father but couldn't. I wanted to tell them about being in love so much. But after what my father said I couldn't.

MILES

You decide to hide the engagement from them?

SUSAN

Yeah, I had hoped in time they would soften their views on interracial marriage. But they didn't. It got worse as the civil rights movement got stronger.

MILES

Did you ever tell them about being engaged or later married?

SUSAN

My father no. He died not knowing. My mother noticed I was with child. She asked me where the father was. When I didn't answer she figured it out.

MILES

But before that they thought you stayed in New York just for the job?

SUSAN

Yes, they came to the graduation and went right back home.

MILES

When did you leave my father?

SUSAN

It was six months into the marriage.

MILES

Why did you leave my father? You didn't love him anymore or what?

SUSAN

No, I loved your father very much. The reaction to us dating versus being married were so different.

MILES

How?

SUSAN

Son, the comments and reactions to us being married become to get more cruel and some even dangerous.

MILES

Couldn't you have moved somewhere else?

SUSAN

Where could we move to? New York City was one of the most liberal cities in the country on race.

MILES

So, what was some of the things said or done to make you leave?

SUSAN

We didn't have money for a honeymoon. So after we got married at school we stayed at a local hotel in downtown New York City. When we returned the next day to our apartment there was a note under our door. It read you know that you weren't suppose to marry a white girl. you better run for your life."

MILES

That was horrible. What did you do?

SUSAN

We took the note to the police station to make a report. They joked with your father about whether he was going to take the note's advice.

MILES

So know help there.

SUSAN

Then one day you're father surprised me at work with some flowers. The police was almost called of him for waiting for me in the lobby even though the receptionist knew who he was.

MILES

Maybe, your other coworkers didn't know who he was?

SUSAN

I introduced him to everyone there when we got engaged.

MILES

What did your bass say the next day?

SUSAN

He called me into his office. I worked for a small local newspaper. He said "Did you think of the consequences to our paper of your marriage to a black man? To our sponsors? I told him that I hadn't. He told me that your father could never come on the paper's property again. He muttered some racial slurs when he told me to leave his office.

MILES

Did you get fired?

SUSAN

No, but I should have quit. We really needed the money. I didn't tell your father what my boss said. My immediate supervisor watched me like a hawk. Work became very stressful. The big boss was waiting for something to fire me for.

MILES

I guess Mom that was enough?

SUSAN

From our landlords smiling jokes, to strangers on the streets people's comments began getting to me. By the time I left I was almost two months pregnant without realizing it.

MILES

Maybe that made you more sensitive to them?

SUSAN

Maybe

MILES

Did you just leave or did you tell him?

SUSAN

No, I told him and told him why. He said we could survive it. But I felt we couldn't, I couldn't.

MILES

How did it take it?

SUSAN

Of course he was more angry than anything else. He never begged me to stay. He only asked that I tell his parents. I hesitantly agreed.

MILES

How did they take it?

SUSAN

Strangely they weren't angry at me just really sad for both of us. They said they understood. They said "Son, you don't understand that Susan is new to such cruel, prejudice to her. They understood that it was destroying me inside. They hoped I just needed a break from it.

MILES

Was that all I needed?

SUSAN

I wasn't sure but when I went home my mother was ill. But my father died of a heart attack a month after I got there. My mother had lung cancer. I stayed there to take care of her for six months until she died.

MILES

When did she notice was expecting?

SUSAN

You mean when did she notice I was expecting? It was around my fourth month. She straight out asked me if I was. Then when I told her I yes she was quiet for a long time. Then she said was I trying to tell her about the baby's father before my graduation. I told her yes. She began to tear up. She asked me to give it another chance for the sake of the baby.

MILES

Did you go back?

SUSAN

Yes, but it had been so long since I left. I didn't keep in touch with your father. I knocked on the apartment door. It was in the winter time so I had on a huge coat. It was silence for a minute when he opened the door. "Susan, I didn't think I would ever see you again. You didn't keep in touch at all." Then a woman called from inside. "Honey, whose at the door?" she said. "It's Susan, my first wife." He answered. We three talked briefly. He introduced her as his fiancé. I told him congratulations to them both.

MILES

Why didn't you tell him?

SUSAN

Because he looked so at peace and happy.

MILES

So, what happened next?

I asked them both to see me off to the NYC Port Authority. If I told him he would have wanted us to get back together.

Susan

That was my pre wedding gift to them For them to see me get on that bus. For them to know I was out of their lives for good.

MILES

That was something. You must have loved my dad a lot.

SUSAN

Yes, I did. And when you were born looking only white that was easier to let it be.

MILES

Do you have any regrets?

SUSAN

Yes, I wish I had been stronger from the beginning of our dating and told my parents.

MILES

Do you mind if I find my father?

SUSAN

No, his name is MICHAEL B. I heard he was a sports Journalist for Colorful Sports in NYC. But remember he is a good man and he didn't know. Search your own heart of what to do. A picture of him is in a box in the back of my bedroom closet. There are no more relatives alive on my side. I'm so sorry son. Please forgive me. I'm proud of you.

Susan starts to breathe slower. Monitors going off. Miles jumps up.

MILES (holds his mom, tells her he forgives her –

SUSAN (whispers thank you son,
love you – before she dies)

MILES turns the light off in his bedroom and goes to sleep.

The next morning. Int.-MILES executive office. MILES standing up looking at his degrees and awards on his office wall. MILES gets on his computer. He picks up his phone.

MILES

Can I have the phone number for Colorful Sports Magazine in NYC?....

Can you dial it? Hello, this is MILES KENNEDY, can I speak to Michael B?....(he pauses then hangs up the phone.)

MILES stands up and walks around his room. He picks up the phone again.

MICHAEL (dials the phone)

Hello, my name is MILES KENNEDY. I am a journalist for the New MAGAZINE. I am considering doing an article on the Arista Society of Queens for our Black History Edition. I understand you were in one of their cotillion's back in 1968?

INT-Office of MICHAEL B - He is sitting at his desk.

MICHAEL JONES

Who are you again and what do you want?

MILES

I am a journalist from the New Magazine. I would like to interview you about being in the Arista Society of Queens cotillion back in 1968?

MICHAEL

How did you get my information?

MILES

I contacted Mr. Giles, the cotillion's photographer.

MICHAEL

Oh yeah, Mr. Giles is still around. You have all your credentials Mr. Miles Kennedy?

MILES

Yes, our secretary can fax them right to your office immediately or if you prefer our courier service.

MICHAEL

I like to give another journalist the benefit of the doubt. When do you need this information?

MILES

In about a month or two.

MICHAEL

My schedule is tied up for the rest of this month. But how about the first Tuesday of next month about 10:00am. Your office or mine?

MILES

Have you been to any of the new restaurants at Grand Central Station?

MICHAEL

No

MILES

Well, I can fax you over the menu to the Michael Z Restaurant along with my credentials.

MICHAEL

Are you kidding?

MILES

Do you want me to send over our car for you around 9:00a.m.? Or for an early breakfast or late lunch?

MICHAEL

No, I'll see you at the restaurant at 10:00a.m. Reservations will be under the New Magazine, right?

MILES

Yes, and thank you. See you then. Bye

MICHAEL

Bye

MILES sat down in his office. He pulled the picture of his father out of his desk drawer. He wiped the tear that rolled down his face as he thought of his mother.

MICHAEL stood up in his office. Ring his phone rang. He answered it.

MICHAEL

Hello

IDA (his wife)

Hello, how's your day going?

MICHAEL

I don't know, maybe strangely.

IDA

What's wrong honey?

MICHAEL

He wants to write a story on the Arista Society of Queens Cotillion I was in back in 1968.

IDA

What's so strange about that?

MICHAEL

I don't know. It was something in his voice.

IDA

Was that some about the time you were dating your first wife?

MICHAEL

No, that was a few years before I met her. I was a senior in high school in the cotillion. Why?

IDA

I don't know. It was just a passing feeling.

The interoffice buzzer goes off in his office.

MILES

Got to go. I'll be home on time for dinner. Bye

IDA

Bye

Time-1968, Empty living room. Worn out couch, chairs and broken down black and white T.V. New is on the TV Suddenly the volume goes up.

NEWS REPORTER (on TV)

This is a special report. Dr. Martin Luther King has just been shot. I repeat Dr. Martin Luther King has just been shot outside his motel room. He is believed to be dead. TV goes black for a moment. Then it comes back on. The reporter is interviewing people standing outside the motel.

NEWS REPORTER (on TV)

How do you feel about Dr. Martin Luther King being shot?

BYSTANDER (on TV)

How do you think I feel as a black person from the deep, deep south? The TV goes black. The TV comes back on to show the funeral procession of Dr. Martin Luther King Jr. TV screen goes black. TV comes back on.

NEWS REPORTER (on TV)

This is a special report. Kennedy has just been shot. I repeat Kennedy has just been shot. He is believed to be severely hurt.

TV screen goes black. TV screen comes back to light. It shows the funeral procession of Kennedy. The room begins to get darker and darker until its pitch black.

Daytime-Ext. NYC 1968-Outside a newsstand. Newspaper say's date-1968. Subway station sign Reads Linden Blvd Station. Two ladies and little girl are standing near the subway entrance.

MILEY CASTLE (early thirties, Deanna's mother)

Wait, Hattie let me make sure I have the address before we get on the subway.

MILEY looks into her pocketbook. She pulls out a piece of paper. Shows it to HATIE

HATIE MCDONALD (early 20's,)

MILEY, we are going to be late.

MILEY

Maybe not. Lately these trains have been moving fast.

DEANA (MILEY's six year old daughter)

Mommy, I'm thirsty.

MILEY

DEANA, we have to get this subway now. I'll get you something to drink as soon as we get there.

INT-Subway System. –DEANA, MILEY and HATIE walk down the stairs and get on the subway. They get off the subway. They walk up the stairs to exit the subway system. The sign outside the subway system reads 42nd street and Broadway.

MILEY (looks at her watch)

We are on time.

HATIE

Yeah, we made much better time by subway than driving.

DEANNA (agitated)

Mom, I'm

MILEY

Okay, the newsstand over there should have some juice.

The three of them walk to the corner newsstand and buy some juices.

MILEY (worried)

Maybe this trip is to long for her.

HATIE

Maybe but you wanted her to see how much hard work went into the cotillion. You just didn't want her to see all the glamour on the day of it.

MILEY

Thanks for reminding me of that cousin.

HATIE

But do you really think we have a chance of getting the famous B Hotel to let us rent one of their ballrooms for the cotillion?

MILEY (laughing)

Well...

HATIE (laughing)

Please don't say it.

MILEY (still laughing)

I have to. Nothing ventured, nothing gained.

DEANNA finishes her juice. She throws the carton in the garbage chute on the street.

DEANNA

Mommy, are we close to it?

MILEY

You see that fancy building across the street?

DEANNA

Yes.

MILEY

Well, we're going in there. It's a big hotel with big fancy rooms for special occasions called ballrooms. We are going there to see if they can rent us one for the cotillion.

DEANNA

Mommy are we really going in there?

MILEY

Yes we are.

The three of them crossed the street to the hotel. The doorman opened the door for them. They went to the front desk.

Interior Hotel-Fancy from ceiling to carpet.

HOTEL EMPLOYEE

Can I help you?

MILEY

Yes, thank you. I have a 11:00 meeting with Mr. Jaccaby.

HOTEL EMPLOYEE (looks in desk book)

Are you sure, I don't see you on the schedule.

MILEY

Is he here? I confirmed it with his assistant just yesterday. Can we wait a few minutes to see if he's just running late?

HOTEL EMPLOYEE (shrugs shoulders)

Suit yourself. You can sit over there and wait.

The three of them take seats furthest away from the hotel's check in desk. The two adults become nervous. The employee makes a phone call taking quietly. In ten minutes two NYC policeman walk in. The employee points to the three. The policeman walk over to the seated three.

Mr. Michael Jaccaby walks into the Hotel. He walks excitedly to the front desk. He is the owner.

MICHAEL JACCABY

Barbara, did my 11:00 appointment come yet?

He looks at her face. Then he looks around at the two policeman walking over to the three seated.

MICHAEL (reaching out his hand)

Excuse me, are you Mrs. Castle? Sorry that I was late.

POLICEMAN 1

You know them? I thought they were here just loitering. That was what we were told.

MICHAEL

No, they're not loitering. Sorry for the mix-up. There here to discuss our hotel Hosting their cotillion this summer.

POLICEMAN 2

You say you're thinking of having these people in your hotel. Some don't like these people being treated like that. You're sure you want to think about doing this? It could be some not so nice consequences?

MICHAEL

I'm sure.

POLICEMAN 1 (agitated voice)

Okay, better watch yourself. No more misunderstandings.

Two policemen leave the hotel. Michael Jaccaby turns to Miley and Hatie extending his hand again.

MICHAEL

Sorry for the misunderstanding. I can assure my employee will be dealt with.

MILEY

Thank you for meeting with us. This is my first cousin, Mrs. Hatie McDonald.

MICHAEL

Nice to meet you Mrs. McDonald.

HATIE

Nice to meet you too. Thank you for helping us with the police.

MICHAEL

It's sad that some people still feel that way. Who's the little girl? I'm sorry she had to hear that. My granddaughter is about her age. (he turns to her) I'm sorry. Are you hungry?

DEANNA (turns to her mother-her mother nods)

Yes

MILEY

This is my daughter DEANNA and she's always hungry. (everyone laughs)

MICHAEL

Sounds like my granddaughter Mary. Well, we just have to go up to my office. I will order lunch for all of us. We can discuss what date you want to have your cotillion here over lunch. You will get a huge discount because of DEANNA's smile.

MILEY (shocked)

What? Did I hear right? We can have the cotillion here?

They take the elevator to the penthouse executive business suites. They talk on the elevator.

MICHAEL (laughing)

I hate prejudice. Those policeman's attitude made my decision.They come out of the elevator. The walk into a beautiful suite in the penthouse.

MICHAEL

Excuse me for a moment. (he picks up the phone) This is Michael in the penthouse I would like two nice hot lunch meals and a very special child's one as soon as possible with beverages. Thank you. (he hangs up the phone) Like I was saying how dare someone try to tell me who I can have in my hotel, imagine that.

MILEY (looks at Hatie)

Imagine

Michael takes a picture out of his desk drawer. He brings it over to them.

MICHAEL

Make yourself at home. This is my granddaughter Mary.

MILEY

She's pretty.

MICHAEL

Thanks but she is to spoiled.

MILEY

Now, I know you are a busy man. We would like June 22nd a Saturday.

MICHAEL

That's fine. Mrs. Castle you spoke so passionately about your cotillion and wanting to help kids have a dream, and for them to accomplish it regardless of their race, income or family situation. I had to listen. And I wanted to meet you. But what got me was that you wanted the best for them and my hotel was the best.

MILEY (laughs)

Mr. Jaccaby I hope that I didn't talk to much. But I know how these kids may feel.

MICHAEL

How? You look like you're doing okay. I ran the background check. Your husband is a doctor, you own your own house in Westchester and you have your own store.

MILEY

Because I didn't grow up like that. I grew up poor. I grew up watching my mother clean another woman's house after my parents divorce. We had a room in that house.

MICHAEL

Oh, I understand now. Well, let me tell you my story.

There was a knock on the door. It was the food. The server brought it in on tray's and tables.

MICHAEL

Everyone dig in. Let me assure you you can have any
ballroom.

MILEY

I am prepared next month to give you a down payment.

MICHAEL

You can but that will not be necessary.

MILEY

Why?

MICHAEL

Because each I'm sure each kid knows the trust and
investment your organization, Community and family
has in them. They will represent you will in my hotel, I
can feel it. I will take the insurance payment if you want
to as part of the final payment. Deal done.

MILEY

Excuse me for saying like this but just like that, no
contract?

MICHAEL

I go by what I feel about the person that I'm doing business with. If I get a negative feel, no piece of paper will bring me any comfort.

HATIE

I don't believe it either. Just like that. Some people may not like it. Why?

MILEY

HATIE

MICHAEL

No, it's all right. That's an understandable question with people's attitude about race today. Just like those policeman downstairs. As you know I am Jewish. I was ten when our small town in Germany was over taken by the new Hitler government. (voice cracking)

HATIE (softly)

You don't have to tell us, I'm so sorry.

MICHAEL (voice stronger)

But I want to tell me. It helps me to tell my story. In Germany at first you loss of jobs for the Jews that didn't leave their country. Then Jewish kids couldn't go to school anymore. Then it changed so drastically and fast.

MICHAEL

Jews were herded like cows to holding locations. Then we were taken to concentration camps. The last time that I saw my parents were on that day. They separated the men, woman and children. I still don't know how I survived. My younger siblings were shot in front of me.

HATIE

I'm so sorry.

MILEY

That's so terrible.

MICHAEL

I'll never forget at the end of the war when the allied troops came in. There was a lot of bombing. The Nazi soldiers locked us in our cells.

HATIE

Please, you don't have to go any further.

MICHAEL

I want you to understand. We thought we would be killed by the bombs Starve to death or freeze to death. United States troops started to get thru. It was a all black army troop that got to us first. One of the officers freed me out of my cell. I was to weak to walk. He carried me all the way back to the rescue point, He gave me his rations with tears in his eyes.

HATIE

I can understand now why you hate prejudice so much.

MICHAEL

Not only done to my people. When I came to the United States I was horrified to see your race treated so badly. It was hard to believe that those black soldiers who risked their lives to save us in Germany so compassionately did not have equal rights in their own country.

HATIE

Yeah, prejudice is something.

MICHAEL

That's why every chance I get to even things out for anyone being discriminated against, I do. I went to Washington with Dr. King.

MILEY

Thank you so much for sharing your story. It means so much to know that you support our kids. Some kids feel they have no value, that they're not as good as other kids and that they have no future to look forward too.

MICHAEL

I understand. But maybe for one day at least they will truly feel special, honored and loved.

HATIE

It is our hope.

MILEY

That is why I brought my daughter with us. I want her to remember this day, this hotel and all the work that went into the cotillion.

MICHAEL

Yes, the next generation

The finished eating. They hugged goodbye.

PRESENT2010--DEANNA closed the cotillion book. The phone rang.

DEANNA

Right. My daughter wants to tag along with us, is that okay?

MILES

Yes, as long as she doesn't interfere with the interview.

DEANNA

She won't. I told her she is only there to observe and not to participate in the interview.

MILES

Okay, see you tomorrow.

DEANNA

Int,. MILES office

MILES leaned back in his chair. The secretary walked into his office.

SECRETARY

You look content.

MILES

Yeah, I'm starting to feel more confident about February's story.

SECRETARY

What's it about?

MILES

It's about an African-American cotillion held in 1968 at a the famous B Hotel.

SECRETARY

That's it.

MILES

What do you mean, that's it?

SECRETARY

What's so special about it? How did you get interested in it? Why are you doing a story about it?

MILES

Oh, first you have to remember what was going on in this country back in 1968. There were civil rights revolutions going on. Schools were just being desegregated in the south. It had to be enforced with national guards in the schools. Blacks were still being found hung up in trees in the south.

SECRETARY

Wow, when did you get so interested in history?

MILES (takes a long breath)

I was researching for a black story for February's black history month article.

SECRETARY

Are you sure that's it? You seem to have taken a personal interest in this story.

MILES

Why do you say that?

SECRETARY

I don't know it's something in your voice.

MILES (laughs nervously)

Okay

SECRETARY

Can I see it before the final cut?

MILES

Of course

The SECRETARY leaves his office. MILES works on his computer for a few minutes. The he straightens up his office and turns off the light to head home.

The next morning. DEANNA's house-Int.-DEANNA and HESSA in the kitchen finishing up breakfast. The phone rings. DEANNA answers it.

DEANNA

HELLO

MILES

Hello, I'm about ten minutes from your house. Are you ready?

DEANNA

Yes, just give a call back when you pull up in front, okay?

MILES

Will do.

In ten minutes MILES calls. DEANNA and HESSA come out.

HESSA

Hello, I'm HESSA (getting into the car)

MILES

Nice to meet you. I'm MILES KENNEDY.

DEANNA

Hello

MILES

Ready for the day?

DEANNA

Yes, I am. Do you have specific questions for Mr. Giles?

MILES

Some, but nothing written in gold.

They get back onto the highway. Headed back to NYC.

DEANNA

Mr. Giles is a very nice man. He likes to talk.

MILES

Great, so I can get a feeling of how it was back then.

HESSA

Are we almost there?

DEANNA

Almost.

They pull off the highway.

MILES

So, DEANNA you use to live around here?

DEANNA

Yes, this is Jamcai Queens. We lived on Williams St.

They pulled up in front of the store. They got out and went in.

MR. GILES

Hello, everyone. Mr. MILES KENNEDY. We talked on the phone.

Nice to meet you in person. I'm EMMANUEL GILES.

MILES

Nice to meet you also. Thank you so much for giving me this interview.

GILES

Your welcome. Hi DEANNA. Why so quiet, little, little Castle. Do you have enough of your middle school graduation pictures?

HESSA

No, I only have a few left. Mom told me I have to be quiet for this interview and not get in the way.

GILES (laughing)

Oh that's all. You were so quiet I thought you were sick.

HESSA makes a face and her mother DEANNA starts to laugh.

MILES

Why did you call her little, little Castle?

Mr. Giles (laughing)

Well, DEANNA was so little when her mother did the cotillion. But her mother had her everywhere she went and at every rehearsal. The orchestra leader, Mr. Wilkes started calling her that.

MILES

And the name kind of stuck, huh? And I guess all the other adults started calling her that too? So her daughter had to be little, little castle right? (laughing)

Mr. Giles (smiling)

Now you're getting it. Saying that name brings back all the fond memories of the cotillion.

MILES

So, why did you agree to be the photographer of the cotillion? And why didn't you charge for your services?

Mr. Giles (paused for a moment)

Because Mrs. Castle presented herself and the purpose of the cotillion a little different than other black cotillions back then.

MILES

How?

Mr. Giles

When she talked about giving the kids there due dignity and respect regardless of where they came from or who their parents were it seemed sincere.

MILES

Anything else?

Mr. Giles

I saw a long intense pain that hadn't healed when she talked about helping the kids in her eyes. It was personal for her. Although she and her husband pulled up in a new Cadillac the first time they came to talk to me. It fit there Westchester address but it didn't really fit them. They both were to humble.

MILES

Why didn't you charge the kids for their individual pictures from the cotillion? The head, black and white block pictures especially.

Mr. Giles

I asked Mrs. Castle who would be helping to sponsor the cotillion. She told me the small black owned businesses and employee unions were the kids were from. That meant from Harlem, The Bronx and here in Queens. It made me feel proud to be black on that day. With all the talk of us only tearing each other down, it was a stand in positivity. It was a sacrifice for each of those struggling businesses. Mrs. Castle had a dream of wrapping those kids in positive support from their community with acknowledgment and love for at least one night. I wanted to help in anyway I could.

MILES

Did you ever find out why it was so personal for Mrs. Castle?

Mr. Giles

Yes, but it's personal. Little Castle is it okay?

DEANNA

Yes

Mr. Giles

She was raised by her mother only after her parents divorced back in the early 1930's back in Alabama. But it only made her stronger, like her mom.

MILES

Wow

Mr. Giles

Here are some of the pictures.

MILES

This is something. Thank you so much Mr. Giles.

MILES shakes MR. Giles hand. DEANNA gives Mr. Giles a hug. Hessa say's goodbye. They walk back outside to the car.

HESSA

Now, where are we going?

DEANNA

We are going to Harlem to meet with the retired president of the H Hospital Black Employees Union that supported the cotillion.

HESSA

They had a union all the way back then?

DEANNA

Yes, surprising huh?

HESSA

Yes

They got back on the highway. They drove over the tribourogh Bridge into Manhattan.

MILES

There is H Hospital. I'd like to drive around the hospital to get a feeling for the neighborhood. The area where people work at.

HESSA

Mom, there's no spaces in front.

DEANNA

It's okay we may have to park a few blocks from the hospital.

HESSA

I don't feel comfortable walking in this neighborhood.

DEANNA

I'll tell you what my friends in the South Bronx told me when I was about your age. "Just mind your business, don't think that you are better than no one else. And you will be all right."

HESSA

Mom, that might have worked back then but things are different now.

(They found parking space around three blocks from the hospital. They walked back.)

DEANNA

Times are different but people are still the same in some ways.

(They show ID at the security window in the apartment complex next to the hospital.)

(They go to the fourth floor on the elevator. DEANNA knocks on the door.)

Mr. Wilson (retired president of Hospital Black Employees Union)

Who is it?

DEANNA

Hi, Mr. Wilson it's DEANNA, my daughter and the reporter from the New

Mr. Wilson (unlocks his door.)

Hello, come on in. You can't be to careful in this neighborhood. Have a seat.

MILES (extends his hand)

Hi, I'm MILES KENNEDY we spoke on the phone. It's nice to meet you.

Mr Wilson

Nice to meet you to. It's been a while, little castle. Sorry I couldn't make it to your mother's funeral. Is this the little one?

DEANNA

I understand. Yes this use to be the little one. Thank you for giving the interview.

Mr. Wilson

My pleasure, what would you like to know Mr. Kennedy?

MILES

Just like that?

Mr. Wilson

Yes son, time is money, even in retirement (laughing)

MILES

As president of the union why did you support the cotillion and have your members support it?

Mr. Wilson

I can tell you right away. The organizers of the cotillion were not rich. The kids in the cotillion came from mostly poor, single parent families who didn't even own formal clothes like a suit or fancy dress. It seemed like a financial impossible thing to do back then in 1968.

MILES

Anything else?

Mr. Wilson

Some of our older men union members came to me a few months before the cotillion. They said "some of the boy's in the cotillion don't have fathers around, do they?" I told them that was true. They said whose going to rent them their tuxedo's, whose going to take them there and show them how to wear their cumber band's? I told them I didn't know.

MILES

What happened?

Mr. Wilson

They went to Mrs. Castle for a list of all the boys without a father around. A male union member volunteered to take each one to get his tuxedo and pay for it if the family couldn't afford it. I will never forget one hardened Youngman's face turn a little softer as he looked at himself in the mirror wearing his tuxedo, and the union member in the background.

MILES

What happened the night of the cotillion?

Mr. Wilson

The boys were cool and smooth. Freda Astaire had nothing on them that night. It was something from the flower girls, the young boy bogglers, the ladies in waiting, the debutants all the way to their escorts. It was a black version of King Arthurs court all the way to the crowing of the Queen and King. Then to the salute of Mr. Wilkes full black orchestra. It was something.

MILES

Do you have any of the rehearsal pictures?

Mr. Wilson

Yes

MILES

Thank you so much. I'm beginning to understand how special this cotillion was.

Mr. Wilson

Well, I think your story will only flow when you feel how special it was from your heart not your mind.

They said goodbye to Mr. Wilson and left.

MILES

Anyone hungry?

HESSA

Yes, I'm starving.

They walked to a restaurant in the area. After they ate they went back to the car.

MILES

While were here I'll see if the owner of the jazz club that was a sponsor is available for a interview. I think it was the sugar something jazz connect.

HESSA

Is it far?

DEANNA

He lives in your grandparents old stomping ground, the Sugar Hill section of Harlem.

MILES

Was that famous for something?

HESSA

Don't you live in NYC? And aren't you a news journalist?

DEANNA

HESSA that's...

MILES

No, she's right. I should know these things but I don't. I wasn't born in New York at all. Seems strange since I've been working here for a long time. But here we are. He said he had a few minutes. They got out the car.

Mr. Biltmore (Former Jazz Owner,
standing outside club)

DEANNA you still have that little Castle face. And the little, little Castle, You must be MILES KENNEDY the

news reporter from the New Y I just spoke to. Hi. You'll
come on in.

MILES

Nice to meet you Mr. Biltmore.

Mr. Biltmore

Nice to meet you too. The club closed a few years ago.
But I still have the keys to it. I'll give you a tour of it. And
I'll answer your questions about the cotillion. How's that?

Mr. Biltmore

This is where the music was played from. Mr. Kennedy
what do you want to know?

MILES

What made you want to buy a gold page in the souvenir
journal? It wasn't cheap I heard.

Mr. Biltmore

First I was around to see the organizers plan it from the
beginning.

MILES

What do you mean?

Mr. Biltmore

I was good friends with the owner of the A Theatre back then.

MILES

The famous A Theatre?

HESSA

I'm surprised you know about that.

DEANNA (very agitated)

HESSA that's enough.

Mr. Biltmore

Well, we were all just making it back then. My friend got so tired of hearing about black artists not being able to play in some places. He decided to scrap up some pennies, dimes and singles to first rent a place. Then when it became successful he was able to buy the building.

MILES

How did the owner get involved in the cotillion?

Mr. Biltmore

I was standing there when Mrs. Castle and her cousin came to the office of the A. They wanted a singer for their cotillion. They wanted to know how to get in touch with a runner up from the last week's amateur night. He had sung My Cherrie A.

MILES

So did he?

Mr. Biltmore

Yes, after first getting the permission of the singer.

MILES

So is that why you bought the gold page, sold tickets for the cotillion and gave them free advertisement.

Mr. Biltmore

Yes, and I was impressed that the Arista Society of Queens got the famous Wilkes Orchestral to play.

MILES

Why were you so surprised?

Mr. Biltmore

Because Mr. Wilkes himself was known to have a very high standard of where and to whom he let his orchestra play for. Some of those kids never even heard of a waltz, let alone know how to dance it.

MILES

So, Mr. Wilkes risked his reputation as a orchestra leader and such?

Mr. Biltmore

Yes, the possibility of the cotillion being a flop was there..

MILES

But it wasn't. I heard it was one of the most elegant, classy presentation of young people ever.

Mr. Biltmore

Yes it was. I was there. Look at these pictures. Look at the faces of the kids. Look at the pride in the faces of the audience. Mr. Wilkes personally taught all the boys how to waltz, and how to be a gentleman in escorting the debutants. The Opelia Charm school taught the girls how to be ladies and how to do the formal curtsy from England.

MILES

That's some investment everyone made.

Mr. Biltmore (turning to DEANNA Laughing)

DEANNA you remember, Mr. Wilkes, left foot Castle?

DEANNA (laughing)

Yes, I sure do.

MILES

What's that all about?

Mr. Biltmore

DEANNA would try to imitate the debutant doing the waltz. But she would be start with the wrong foot. It was usually the right instead of the left. I don't know how Mr. Wilkes noticed with all he had to do. But he would yell out left foot castle to her.

MILES (smiling)

Did you ever get it?

DEANNA

No, still to this day I can't waltz. But I developed a love for dance. Was offered to train with a professional group in college but my father said no, education first. But I have no complaints.

MILES

So the family got people who believed in the dream and the kids to be a part of the cotillion.

Mr. Biltmore

Now, you're getting it. Now you have to ask yourself if you have a dream about how this story is received or is it just another article?

MILES

Good point, I'll let you know.

Mr. Biltmore

I want a prepublised copy too.

MILES (shakes his hand)

You'll have one. Thanks for the interview.

They walk back out of the jazz club. MILES is walking slowly thinking about all he has learned.

Miles takes DEANNA and HESSA home. Then he goes to his home.

The next day. INT_MILES OFFICE-MORNING

MILES typing up some of the notes to the interview on his computer. Secretary walks into office.

SECRETARY

What are you so happy about today?

MILES

Oh, nothing.

SECRETARY

Well, nothing sure put a smile on your face early in the morning.

MILES (laughs)

Yeah.

SECRETARY leaves the office shaking her head. MILES works thru lunch. His phone rings.

MILES

Hello

DEANNA (hear her but don't see her)

How do you think the interviews went?

MILES

They went better than expected. It was great that you could come with me. I think that them seeing you reminded them of your mother and the cotillion. It brought back the memories of it.

DEANNA

Yeah, I felt the same way. It was nice seeing them.

BUZZER on the interoffice phone rings.

MILES

DEANNA, Can you hold a minute?

DEANNA

Yes

MILES answers interoffice call-

MILES

Yes

SECRETARY

The boss just walked by. He wants you to stop by to see him before you leave for the day.

MILES

Why?

SECRETARY

My guess is he wants to see how your story is going. He noticed you looked happy today.

MILES (mumbled)

Okay, thanks.

He switched to his phone–

MILES

Hello DEANNA that might have been trouble.

DEANNA

What do you mean?

MILES

He doesn't usually ask to see me about my stories this soon.

DEANNA

Who?

MILES

I'm sorry my boss. My boss just requested my presence in his office before I leave for the day.

DEANNA

MILES, can I trust you to hold to the positive portrayal of the cotillion?

MILES

Yes

DEANNA

What if he say's change it or your job?

MILES

Then I'll take the story with me to my next job.

DEANNA

That's a little much. Why would you do that?

MILES

I can't tell you all of it just yet, but this story is personal. My mother who just died six months ago knew someone in the cotillion okay. It's personal that I do the story right.

DEANNA

I'm sorry about your mother. And I like to hear the rest of it when you're ready. But now I believe you will do the story right.

Miles walks out of his office. He walks into the area outside of his boss's office. He stops for a moment. Miles knocks on his boss's door.

MILES's Boss (inside his office)

Come in

MILES walks inside the office.

MILES's Boss

What's going on MILES? Since when have you been so excited about a black human interest story?

MILES

What are you talking about?

MILES's Boss

Many of your coworkers and I have noticed your excitement about this story?

MILES

Well, it's a good story. It might get me the Jewel's Journalism Award.

MILES's Boss

Oh, that is what it's about. MILES don't you have enough awards yet?

MILES (laughing)

You told me that you can never have enough of them.

MILES boss stands up from his desk chair. He shakes MILES hand.

MILES's boss

Yes I did. Don't try too hard. You'll wear out before 40.

MILES takes a deep breath as he leaves his boss's office. He goes back to his office. He turns his light off. He drives to his home. He picks up his phone in his living room.

MILES

Hello

DEANNA

Hello, is everything all right?

MILES

Yes, everything is all right. How about next week to interview the remaining people?

DEANNA

That sounds great but we will be one person short.

MILES

What happened?

DEANNA

HESSA was to worn out. She didn't realize that organizing the cotillion was so involved. She begged me to take notes for her. She said she would make diner for a whole week. (Laughing)

MILES (laughing)

That sound like a good trade of to me.

DEANNA

I agree.

MILES

See you next week.

DEANNA

Okay

MILES pulls up in front of DEANNA's house. He rings the doorbell. DEANNA comes right out. They both get into the car.

DEANNA

So who are we interviewing first.?

MILES

Mrs. Carretta on Houston Street in lower Manhattan. She's your father's first cousin, right?

DEANNA

Yes. I haven't talked to her in a while. She stay's so busy.

They find a parking space right in front of the building project. They go to the tenth floor.

DEANNA knocks on the door.

CARRETTA

Who is it?

DEANNA

It's DEANNA, Aunt Carretta and Mr. Kennedy from the New Magazine

CARRETTA (opening the door)

Hey baby good to see you. (giving her a hug) Nice to meet you Mr. Kennedy.

MILES

Nice to meet you. And thank you for giving me the interview.

CARRETTA

Now what do you want to know about the cotillion?

MILES

You were a maid in waiting in the cotillion, right?

CARRETTA

Yes

MILES

What made you want to be in the cotillion?

CARRETTA

For two reasons mostly. The first reason is why DEANNA's mother wanted to do the Cotillion. The second was because it was a family thing.

MILES

Wasn't the reason DEANNA's mother wanted to present the kids in a dignified way?

CARRETTA

Yes it was but a specific thing happened that started it all.

MILES

What?

CARRETTA

Do you mind if it's in the story, DEANNA?

DEANNA

Now, you know DEANNA's mother's first cousin Hatie was a teacher. She taught in one of those fancy private high schools. The teachers and students were mostly white back in 1968. One day a teacher walked past one of the honor roll black students and laughed at her studying in the lunchroom. She said "why are you studying so much, you'll probably end up like a domestic like your people.".

MILES

What, that's terrible. DEANNA were you there when your aunt told your mother?

DEANNA

Yes, I was in my mother's store in Harlem. It was a half day at school. Aunt Hattie came in the store very upset. She told my mother what the teacher said to the student. The student refused to go back to school the next day. The other black students wanted to vandalize the school in protest.

MILES

Did they?

DEANNA

No, my aunt promised she would do something about it. She said she would talk to the administrator of the school about it.

MILES

What happened?

DEANNA

He called in the teacher to his office. The teacher said she was just joking. She also said that the student wouldn't survive life without a sense of humor. But the black students were still about to revolt and risk their graduating that year.

MILES

So what happened?

DEANNA

My aunt asked my mother to tell the students her story. She asked her to tell about being raised by a single parent who happened to be a maid in a white woman's house. She told her that maybe she could save the students from jeopardizing their high school diploma and being arrested for vandalizing of the school.

MILES

Did it work?

DEANNA

When we pulled up in a new Cadillac, doctors plates it was a start in believing you can defy the odds I guess. But what did it was my mothers made us kids go outside. She talked one on one with the parents.

MILES

What happened?

DEANNA

She told them, like she told us a million times, with God all is possible.

MILES

So, why the cotillion?

DEANNA

I heard that it brought back the pain of the treatment of being poor and black as a child. She was discouraged that in NY in the late 1960's it was still going on. She wanted one day kids from where she came from economically were treated fairly. And she was sick and tired of the only portrayal of blacks was one of tearing each other down.

MILES

That's something.

DEANNA

Yeah, she said if it wasn't for blacks helping each other during slavery no one would have made it thru that and the Jim Crow days.

CARRETTA

And once MILEY put her mind on something it was all over. When I told my neighbors about the cotillion they wanted to help. One from Mexico insisted on making the table decorations. Another from Brazil got the debutants a good deal on their shoes. My friend from Puerto Rico next door sold tickets at her job.

MILES

I don't know how to ask this?

CARRETTA

Just ask it.

MILES

It wasn't just black people who supported the cotillion?

CARRETTA

Oh no, from the owner of the B Hotel to all the individuals who paid for their names to be in the souvenir journal.

MILES

This is turning out to be some story,

CARRETTA

Just make sure no one pressures you to write it differently.

MILES

I wont.

CARRETTA

For some reason I believe you won't. Anything else?

MILES

No, thank you so much.

DEANNA and MILES said there goodbyes. Got back into the car.

MILES

Does your daughter know all of this?

DEANNA

Not as deeply as she should. But what she does know is not appreciated.

MILES

Maybe

DEANNA

Are you all right?

MILES

I am. How do I interview the former first black woman ambassador of the state of New York State? Of any state for that matter?

DEANNA

Just be kind and respectful like you were to the other interviews.

They drive to the gated community of starlet city in Staten Island. They go thru the security check. They go to her front door and knock.

Mrs. Carlene Chiasm (opens the door)

Little Castle, you still look the same, you look so much like your mom. Come on in. Mr. Kennedy from the New Magazine, nice to meet you.

They sit down on her couch in the living room.

Ms. Chiasm

So, Mr. Kennedy what would you like to know?

MILES

Do you mind if I tape this interview?

Ms. Chiasm

Yes I do. You can just take notes.

MILES

I understand. My first question is why did you decide to be part of this cotillion? Then why be Mistress of ceremonies?

Ms. Chiasm

That is a good question. Let me think back for a moment. I wasn't appointed yet as Ambassador but I was in the running.

MILES

Wasn't you afraid of something looking unfavorably on you and you losing the appointment?

Ms. Chiasm

I wasn't afraid but very much aware of it.

There was a lot of pressure to distance myself from anything or anyone that maybe considered negative by public opinion. Then someone told me to be part of the cotillion would look like a publicity stunt. It might look like was exploiting poor people.

MILES

Wow, that was a hard position to be in. So what made you decide?

Ms. Chiasm

DEANNA's mother asked me to meet with her about the cotillion. I kept telling her by phone I was to busy. She was so persistent. Finally she said if I gave her one afternoon of my time and decided not to be in it, she would leave me alone. I agreed.

MILES

What happened?

Ms. Chiasm

She took me to meet the black student at her cousin's school who almost quit because of what a teacher said. Then she took me to her house in White Plains were "they" said blacks would never live. She told me of her humble beginnings.

MILES

What?

Ms. Chiasm

Yes, she was very dramatic to make her point.

MILES

Did she make her point to you?

Ms. Chiasm

Yes, she asked me if I was born with a silver spoon or like her?

MILES

She was bold.

Ms. Chiasm

Bold wasn't the word for it. Then she shifted. She begged me to represent for every black girl or boy who were told by word, deed or attitude that they were born nothing, grew up as nothing and will never be anything because of race and poverty, and sometimes single parent home that that is not true. Stand at the cotillion she said to show the stereotypes wrong. Show that hard work, determination and faith can do something positive.

MILES

That must have been powerful

Ms. Chiasm

We both had tears in our eyes. She said "Ms. Chiasm the pain never really goes all away but if you have one person that really believes in you, you can make it. I'm asking you to believe in these kids. I'm asking you to be that one person."

MILES

What did you say after that?

Ms. Chiasm

After that I not only wanted to be a part of it, but Mistress of Ceremonies. Ironically, I was appointed a few months after the cotillion.

MILES

Coincidence maybe?

Ms. Chiasm

No, the Governor of New York told me he received several letters from parents of some of the kids in the cotillion recommending me for the appointment. But one letter from one of the kids made him decide.

MILES

What did the letter say, it it's not to personal?

Ms. Chiasm

The letters from the parents were general saying they appreciated me encouraging their children with school, looking for jobs or going to college after high school graduation. The debutants letter was deep and detailed. She said she heard of cotillions for the rich black girls. But when I came to their rehearsal it blew her mind. And when I told them of being their mistress of ceremony she felt validated as a human being. Then when I looked at all of them in the eyes at one of the practices at Andrew Jackson High School to tell them "Do not let anyone make you feel like an inferior creation of God. Feel like you are on of the beautiful variety of flowers in his garden." It was over. The hopelessness started going away.

MILES

What did the Governor say?

Ms. Chiasm

He said that the reason he appointed me was I gave hope to some who had lost theirs. There was silence in the room for a moment. DEANNA wiped her eyes with tissue. They said there goodbyes with a hug. DEANNA and MILES got back into the car.

MILES

Your mother had a lot of love.

DEANNA (laughing)

But my mother was so strict growing up. She would say "I'd rather you hate me now, and love me later than love me now and hate me later.

MILES

And do you love her now?

DEANNA

Extremely, every second of the day.

MILES

Are you up for another interview?

DEANNA

Just one more for the day.

MILES picks up his mobile phone and makes a call.

MILES

Let's see if the Debutant Queen on the 1968 cotillion can spare a few minutes. Hello, can I speak to Dr. Venetia Hess please?....This is Mr. Kennedy from the New Yes, I will hold.....

L Hill Hospital, Oncology Department-Private office of Dr. Hess. She picks up her desk phone.

Dr. Hess

Mr. Kennedy how are you?

MILES

I'm good thanks for calling. Mrs Deanna Castle and I just finished interviewing someone for the cotillion article. I wanted to know if you could spare a few minutes this afternoon to be interviewed?

Dr. Hess

Surprisingly, I do. In about a hour from now. Just ask at the receptionist desk how to get to my office. See you then.

MILES

Thank you so much.

MILES turns to DEANNA. He pulls out the parking space.

MILES

That worked out well. We have time to grab something to eat,

DEANNA

That's a good idea.

MILES and DEANNA find a fast food place to pull into. They have lunch. Then back onto the highway to the Bronx to Lennox Hill Hospital. They find a space near the hospital and talk as they're walking to it.

MILES

This is something. A doctor who is head of the oncology makes time for an interview within an hour on the spur of the moment. That's amazing. That's a story in itself.

DEANNA

She's still grateful, I guess.

MILES

More than grateful. I hear it in her voice. There's a lot of love for your mother and what was given to those kids back then thru the cotillion.

MILES

I'm starting to feel it. And this is about something over thirty years later.

DEANNA (laughing)

Why MILES you're not getting caught up in the emotions of the cotillion are you?

MILES (laughing)

No, I can't do that. After all I'm a seasoned journalist.

DEANNA (laughing)

If you say so.

They arrive at the receptionist desk for Dr. Hess in the Oncology Department.

DEANNA

Hello, I'm Mrs. Castle and this is Mr. Kennedy we have an appointment with Dr. Hess.

Receptionist. (gets up from her seat)

Yes, Dr. Hess is expecting you. Come right this way.

She shows them thru double doors right to the office. She knocks on the door.

Dr. Hess

Come in

DEANNA

Hello, Dr. Hess how are you? This is Mr. Kennedy from the New ???

Dr. Hess (smiling, outstretched hand)

Dr. Hess

DEANNA nice to see you. Nice to meet you in person Mr. Kennedy.

MILES

Thank you for letting me on such short notice. How are you?

Dr. Hess

I'm thankful. My cancer has been in remission for a year now. I just returned to work a few months ago. So, what did you want to ask me about the cotillion?

MILES

Was there any obstacles to being in the cotillion and how did you personally benefit from being in it?

Dr. Hess

Well, first I didn't even want to be in it. I didn't want to wear a evening gown or learn how to waltz. The rehearsal times I felt was a waste of time. I thought DEANNA's mom was trying to turn us into white kids. But DEANNA I heard what you said when your mother came to our apartment to talk to my mom about the cotillion.

DEANNA (laughing)

That was you I said that to.

MILES

What did you say?

DEANNA

I said "But you have to be in the cotillion. You are going to look so pretty in the gown." My mother just gave me that look. That look of grown people are talking here.

MILES

Did that make you want to be in it?

DEANNA

Not really, I had no choice. Mrs. Castle found out I wanted to go to college. She told my mother that the Queen of the cotillion got a college scholarship. So it helped me get to Harvard. And the recommendation letter by Mrs. Chiasm sealed it.

MILES

Anything else?

Dr. Hess

Yes, growing up was hard for our family. My dad died when I was a baby. We had enough of the basics but no extra's. In college when other kids talked about their trips, music lessons, and all the extra's they grew up with, I took out my cotillion journal. It made me not feel so inferior. It made me remember. It made me work hard when I thought of how hard those adults worked to do the cotillion.

MILES

That's powerful.

Phone Buzzer rang. Dr. Hess answered it.

Dr. Hess

Thanks Denise... Sorry surgery is calling I have to go.

MILES

Thank you so much. I will definitely make sure you get a pre published copy of the article.

DEANNA

Thank you and I'm glad you're so much better.

DEANNA and MILES leave the hospital. MILES takes DEANNA home and returns to his home. The next morning-Int-DEANNA's kitchen. DEANNA answers the phone.

DEANNA

Hello

MILES

Hello, are you free to do the last two interviews today?

DEANNA

Yes, about what time?

MILES

Around ten depending on the traffic.

DEANNA

Okay, see you then.

MILES arrives at DEANNA's house. He knocks on the door. DEANNA comes out.

DEANNA

So who are you interviewing today?

MILES

We are going to interview the king of the 1968 cotillion.

DEANNA

Really, you know he is now a New York Y??? pitching coach?

MILES

I was surprised. I couldn't resist asking him could the interview be at Y Stadium. So here we go.

Ext-Y??? Stadium-mid morning. They pull into a parking garage closest to the main ticket office. DEANNA and MILES walk over to the ticket office and ask for Clyde M???. He comes to the office.

DEANNA

Hello, how have you been? This is Mr. Kennedy from the New Magazine.

CLYDE MARTIN

I've been well little Castle. Sorry to hear about your mom's passing. Sorry I couldn't make it. (outstretches his hand) Nice to meet you Mr. Kennedy.

MILES

Nice to meet you too.

CLYDE

Let's go inside to have the interview. I can give you a brief tour as we talk. I only have a few minutes to spare.

(They begin walking thru the inside of the stadium. And up thru the club offices.)

MR. KENNEDY

Did you have any obstacles in being in the cotillion and how did you benefit?

CLYDE

Are you kidding about obstacles? My mother didn't want me to be in the cotillion at first. She had a problem with trust since my dad left her when she was pregnant with me.

MILES

So how was that resolved?

CLYDE

Mrs. Castle convinced her she could trust her. She told her she was raised by her mother only. That in no way would I be treated different than the kids from two parent homes. I still don't know how she did it. When the rehearsals progressed, and word got out that it was real, the community really supported it. My mother started to trust just a little more.

MILES

Anything else?

CLYDE

Mr. Wilkes, the orchestra leader took a personal interest in everyone. He taught the guys how to waltz. The men from the black H Hospital's union made sure we had tuxedos for the cotillion.

MILES

Why was this important?

Clyde

I really didn't care about finishing high school before the cotillion. I thought get the diploma, and the what? But the males mentors in the cotillion encouraged me to get a trade or seek entrance into a community college with the diploma.

MILES

Is that how you benefited from the cotillion?

Clyde

Not only that. Because I was shown the chance at a future the caring came back. I didn't want to get messes up with drugs just before my ship came in.

MILES

So what, happy go thru community school, transfer to university and a break to the minor leagues?

Clyde

No and yes. I joined the baseball team in the community college. I did well. But when I made it to the junior varsity team at the university things got hectic and I couldn't keep up. I started using drugs to give me more energy. I got busted trying to buy some. My mother had no money to bail me out. I asked her to call Mrs. Castle. She gave her the money. I got the second chance of a first offender. But I got hurt in the minor leagues. So I decided to train to be a coach. I was fortunate enough after twenty years coaching in the minor leagues, to now be coaching for the Y. And before my mother died she contacted my father. I met him for the first time.

MILES

All of that from the cotillion?

Clyde

No not all of it.. Some of it. And some just life, healing and time. But I have to go. That gate will take you back to your car. Hey, I want a prepublished copy.

DEANNA and MILES leave the stadium. They make their way to their next interview in the car.

MILES

The next interview might be a little strange. I don't know where it might end up. I have something to confide in you since we seem to becoming friends. The person that my mother knew in your family's cotillion back in 1968 was my father.

DEANNA (shocked)

That's impossible because all the young men were black.

MILES

Exactly, my mother told me six months ago before she died my father was black. She told me little about him all my life, but not that. She told me they were married but she left because of the harassment of others. That's when she discovered she was pregnant. She never told him. They got divorced and everything without him even knowing I was conceived. I grew up assuming he was white just like my mom.

DEANNA

Where did you grow up?

MILES

A small town. My parents met at C School of Journalism. So the man I'm about to interview is my father. He is also a journalist. He is remarried with grown children.

DEANNA

Are you sure you want me to go on this interview with you?

MILES

Yes, it will help me keep focused on my work, interviewing for the article.

DEANNA

What are you going to do? Are you going to tell him?

MILES

I don't know. My mother said he was a good man. She said my heart would lead me to do the right thing.

There was silence in the car as they headed to his house. They pulled up to his house in the Bronx. They parked in front and knocked on the door.

MICHAEL B (he opened the door)

Hello, I'm Michael B.. You must be Mrs. Castle's daughter. And you are Miles Kennedy from the New Magazine right?

DEANNA (looking at Miles for a minute)

Yes, it's been a long time since the cotillion. How have you been?

MICHAEL

Well, can't complain. Sorry to hear about your mother. You'll come on in. This is my wife IDA. IDA CAROL this is Deanna Castle, Mrs. Castle daughter from the cotillion and Miles Kennedy from the New

IDA CAROL (motioning with her hand)

Nice to meet you. You'll sit down and make yourself comfortable. Would you like some lemonade?

MILES

Yes, that would be nice.

Deanna

Yes, thank you.

Michael

Better watch out, my wife is a match maker. And since you have no kids, with a good job you're a good catch for some of her single friends.

IDA CAROL

Michael you need to stop, my matches to turn out well though.

Michael (laughing)

Yeah some of them. But anyway, Michael what did you want to ask me about the cotillion?

MILES

How did you benefit from being in the cotillion?

Michael

Well, in my senior year my grades were slipping badly. I started hanging out with the wrong crowd. My parents insisted I be in the cotillion to keep me out of trouble. With all the rehearsals, selling tickets and journal space my time was occupied.

MILES

So, what happened to help you?

Michael

I was surprised by the support the cotillion got. I wrote an essay about it for my English class. My teacher entered it in for a college scholarship. It won and I decided to go to college and major in journalism.

MILES

And now?

Michael

Now I'm getting to retire from a long career of over forty years that I love and have been blessed to have done well in. Some of the people I met in the cotillion have kept in touch with. They encouraged me thru some tough times in college, job hunting and after a divorce. But I learned a lot from being in the cotillion.

Miles

Thanks for sharing this with me.

IDA

Where are you originally from, I hear your accent?

Miles

I was born in Iowa City, Iowa. I came to New York to go to C University School of Journalism.

IDA

That's something, so did Michael. His first wife was from Iowa too.

Miles (standing up)

What a coincidence. I'll make sure you both get a pre publisher's copy. I have to try to beat the traffic and get Deanna back to White Plains. But thank you both for being so hospitable.

Michael

Anytime. And if you ever need any job advice from a oldster you can call me.

Miles (fought back tears)

Thanks but you're not old. (They shook hands goodbye and got back into the car. Miles took Deanna home. There was silence until Deanna house.)

Three months later-Into-Miles Office. Mid-morning, Miles sitting at his desk looking at the cotillion journal. The phone rings.

MILES

Hello, Mr. Giles....I'm glad you like it. (a beep on the phone.) I have another phone call bye. Hello

MICHAEL (at his office –sport journal magazine)

Michael here. You captured the emotions of the cotillion, great work. Don't be a stranger. Got to go. Bye.

MILES

Thanks Bye…(another phone call)….Hello

Carreta (in her apartment on Houston St.)

Miles you're a man of your word. You told the story right. I loved it. (Beep)

I have to go. If you want some soul food come visit with Deanna. Bye

Int–Deanna's kitchen. Deanna's making diner. Hessa comes in from school–happy.

HESSA–(yelling)

Mom. Mom I got an A on my oral report about the cotillion.

DEANNA (smiling, giving Hessa a hug)

That's great.

HESSA

Mom I get it about the cotillion too. It tried to make people feel good about themselves.

A year later. Miles sitting at his desk in his office he opens up a card from his mail. It read:

YOU ARE CORDIALLY INVITED TO THE FIRST REUNION OF THE ARISTA SOCIETY OF QUEENS AT THE B HOTEL IN NEW YORK, NEW YORK on SATURDAY JUNE 22, 2020.-LA QUI PARLE BALLROOM

Printed in the United States
By Bookmasters